Scourged Vein

Alaric Maison

Published by Alaric Maison, 2024.

This is a work of fiction. Similarities to real people, places, or events are entirely coincidental.

SCOURGED VEIN

First edition. July 12, 2024.

Copyright © 2024 Alaric Maison.

ISBN: 979-8230712763

Written by Alaric Maison.

Chapter 1

"Put it away. Eyes on whoever's talking, and if he speaks to you, don't say more than you have to."

As Theo's family members sat down around the table, his mother's whisper reached his ear under their lively voices.

Though being told to put his phone away like an unruly child wasn't exactly pleasant, Audrey only spoke out of love and concern. He knew that.

"Theodore." A man's voice boomed over the others, quieting the whole room. His hair was slick and short. A deep brown that could easily be mistaken for black if you never got close enough to check. Just like Theo.

Beads of sweat gathered on his skin.

"Why don't you sit next to me?" He spoke again, a thin smile on his lips. It never quite reached his eyes, but their grandparents and aunts were none the wiser. It was no use saying no to the hulking shape that was his brother. Silas.

"Sure..."

Satisfied, his gaze finally left Theo once he sat down

The others were speaking amongst themselves again as they shared the food bowls.

Even though his mother was sitting next to him and he only had to gather food for his plate, there was an uncomfortable stuffiness in the air that he needed to contend with.

"So, Theodore, now that Silas hasn't brought a new girlfriend to our reunion for once, isn't it finally your turn?" One of Theo's aunts raised her glass, her eyes intently on him.

A shiver ran down Theo's spine. But before he could respond, Silas cut him off.

"Hey, now. You didn't have to bring that up. And there's no need to rush him; it'll come eventually."

What Theo would normally have considered a nice gesture couldn't be further from it. He had known Silas his entire life. This was his older brother, after all. There was no reason to distract them from the question other than to get far away from what Silas considered an 'uncomfortable' sexual orientation. Wouldn't want to risk Theo bringing it up.

It took their aunt a second to conjure up her words. That didn't sit well with her. Talking for others wasn't exactly something you'd put past him, though.

"Ah, I suppose you're right. Putting your career first is a very valid choice too."

Theo's knife was slipping from between his fingers. He clutched it with a shaky grip, turning his attention to the candle standing straight ahead on the table when Silas's gaze returned to him.

"A very good point. How's that going, by the way? Still working at that little gas station?"

Oh, how Theo wished he could give him some snarky comeback. But every part of him was fighting against it. Why was it so damn hard?

"Of course. It's a nice, quiet place."

"Uh-huh. Right. Must get pretty lonely out there. I still wonder why you chose to work so far from the city."

"Devin, he—"

"Actually... I don't really care."

Everyone else had gone silent again. Theo's mother shifted uncomfortably in her chair.

"Silas... Pass the salad bowl, please."

He squinted at her, but eventually obliged. Theo was getting tired of Audrey's few light attempts to deal with his brother. When was she going to decide to actually parent him? It was frustrating, yet he couldn't help but blame himself too. It shouldn't be that hard to stand up for yourself, even just a little bit. Right?

As dinner continued, some small talk started cropping up here and there. Theo kept debating over and over in his head whether staying at the table was worth it anymore. He needed air.

At the same time, drawing attention to himself by getting up was the last thing he wanted. So, he'd have to survive another grueling hour at the very least.

Salvation.

"It'll take a bit to get the dessert ready, so why don't we take a break?" Audrey smiled as she got up from her chair.

Everyone followed suit, spreading out into the living room. Theo's grandparents sat down by the television; one of his aunts went out for some fresh air; and his mother headed to the kitchen. Silas was still sitting down across from Theo's other aunt, but neither of them said a word.

Theo couldn't stay there any longer. He was headed in the exact opposite direction of the others; the basement.

So unfamiliar. Yet, its structure still brought him some nostalgia. Though his former bedroom was only used for storage purposes now, he couldn't forget everything that had happened here.

All the ways Silas wanted to prove he knew better. The guys Theo only brought here to quell the way his family made him feel. And the eventual consequences of that.

"Reminiscing? I can only hope you remember the useful things I taught you."

The arrogant voice brought Theo back to reality.

"I... No... I don't remember much."

Theo tried his best to ease the tension Silas was purposefully creating.

"Oh, please. Stop acting so damn coy. It's sickening."

"This is ridiculous..."

Silas lit up.

"What's ridiculous is the absolute state you're in."

Theo took a step away from him. He was just trying to get a favorable reaction out of him now.

"I understand that you're worried, but I'm fine." He was trembling slightly.

Silas furrowed his brows, clearly not satisfied.

"You fu—"

"Boys. Dessert's ready." Audrey appeared from the hole leading into the basement. Though she addressed both, her glare remained locked on Silas.

"Okay. Thank you." There was no joy behind those words.

With a sigh, he pushed past her and disappeared up the stairs.

Now that it was just Theo and his mother, the silence hung even heavier. There was no tension, just... A hollow feeling.

"I'm sure what you made is tasty, but... I think I'm going to go."

"You know what they're going to think."

"Yes. So, can I leave?"

"Of course. Want to leave through here instead of the front door? I'll get your jacket for you."

"No, it's fine. I'll say goodbye."

Her mouth was stretched in a thin line. She wanted to interject but didn't.

"Alright."

As they returned to the living room, the voices of her guests grew louder. Two of them stood out among the others. They came from Theo's grandfather and Silas.

It became more clear what they were discussing the closer Audrey and Theo got, and unsurprisingly, they were as usual agreeing on some tired old opinions every other family member had probably gotten sick of by now. Their need to show off what great and correct men they were was apparently evergreen. It always included some outdated traits and stereotypes.

"Sorry everyone, but I have to get going. It's been fun, though."

Silas's cold eyes landed on him. Surprisingly, he didn't throw in a stray comment this time.

The others, however, all gave their polite goodbyes as Theo left for the main entrance. He grabbed his jacket off the coat rack and headed outside.

There was no doubt they'd be expressing uncalled-for opinions of him with each other afterward, but he'd much rather let that play out than stay there.

Briar was waiting patiently for his owner, after all. At least, as much as a cat could.

The sun shone through the store's low front windows, its glaring strays going right for Theo's eyes.

He stood silently behind the store's counter, unbothered.

That meant his shift was almost over.

"You've been moping all day, Theo. What's going on?"

A man with auburn hair stepped out from the doorway leading to the storage area. He carried a box of food products in his arms.

"Just family stuff. Dinner went as well as you would expect. I'm sure you're tired of hearing about it by now." Theo leaned on his elbows, struggling to hold his head up.

His good friend and coworker Devin slipped past him, heading for the shelves stocked with snacks, drinks, and everyday necessities.

"I would say yes, but I kind of enjoy seeing the irritated side of you. That doesn't happen nearly enough."

Theo chuckled. His eyes darted to the door as a bell noise rang above it. Their new customer pushed it open with haste and went right in Devin's direction.

The man said nothing as he yanked a bag off the shelf he stood in front of. Devin took a step back in surprise, making eye contact with Theo at that moment.

He had many times before described exactly how he felt in those scenarios to Theo. He saw everything he needed in that look.

Coming up to the counter, the guy glared at him as he slammed a few coins down on the wooden surface.

Theo placed them in the cash register, giving him a barely noticeable smile.

"Thank you. Need anything else?"

"Does it fucking look like I do?"

Devin squinted, his gaze directed solely at Theo. But he didn't know what to do. What it meant.

"Uh, no, sorry."

With a huff, he turned around and left the two in silence.

"Well, if that wasn't some unnecessary aggression,"

Perhaps as a form of coping mechanism; all Theo did was laugh nervously.

He looked out the front door. A pair of backlit but familiar dark shapes came into view.

"We're done for today."

Following Theo's gaze, Devin let out a relieved sigh.

"Great." He passed the counter and slipped into the back area.

As the bell rang once again, a man and a woman entered the store.

"Hi, guys."

But, right as the two made it to the table, they walked past him without a word. The man only spared him one glance, but the woman at least waved in his direction.

Theo never really could figure those two out. And considering they didn't bother with him, that probably wasn't going to happen any time soon.

They disappeared into the back.

After getting a moment to gather himself, Theo followed in after them. It was finally time to head home; to the city.

A golden glow traced the edge of Theo's car as it stood by itself in the parking lot. An asphalted area surrounded by trees of mostly the pine variety.

He took in the air around him, which carried a mix of fresh gasoline and a hint of warm, baked goods coming from the store he just left.

"Want to go to the bar?" Devin's voice came from behind him.

It would be nice to wind down with him.

"Oh, absolutely. I could use that. I gotta stop by at home to feed Briar, though."

"I'll come with."

Devin opened the door of Theo's car and got into the passenger seat.

As Theo joined his friend and started it up, he gave him a smug side glance.

"One of these days I'm going to be passed for some reason when we have to drive, and you'll wish you had a driver's license."

"Hah. I'll manage the embarrassment of dragging you into a bus. Thank you very much."

"Will you?"

Though Theo joked, there was a certain sincerity to his tone that made Devin scrunch up his nose.

"...I miss Briar."

It was better to leave this alone.

Once inside Theo's apartment, it didn't take long before a little black shape came to the door. Gleaming, yellow eyes stared up at them. The sight made Devin's face instantly light up.

"It's been too long, friend."

Briar brushed its slender body against his leg. As he bent down to pet him, Briar purred in satisfaction.

"He's kind of making me want to visit the zoo again. It's been a while."

Theo slid past him through the tiny entrance hall.

"You'll make him envious of all your new stories of bigger cats."

An open kitchen stood by the end of the living room the hall led to. Quite the compact place.

A soft hum came from the refrigerator in the background, mixing with the occasional city sounds filtering through the windows.

"There's no one bigger than you, Briar." When he tilted his face closer, the purring animal actually rubbed its cheek against his.

There was no sight greater than that.

"You guys are too cute. It's almost annoying."

Devin looked up at him with a wide grin.

"Speaking of envy."

A pout.

"I'll get him some food, then we'll go."

The local bar had a cozy yet grungy nightlife feel. The air was a mix of spilled beer, worn leather, and a faint trace of cigarette smoke. Dim, colorful lights cast a warm glow over them.

"I'll get us some beer." As Theo pulled his wallet out, Devin gave him a quick nod.

He then headed off to the bar counter.

Mismatched chairs and barstools surrounded him. The wooden bar top, though slightly sticky in places, felt familiar and well-used.

Once Theo had given his order and the bartender was turned around, getting it ready, he observed the other patrons standing near him. A bit further back stood someone you'd have to try hard to look away from.

Short and styled, brown hair. Black shirt, with its sleeves rolled up, practically hugging his body.

Not bad.

"Theo."

He froze as a whisper came from behind. The man snatched up both glasses and leaned closer, squinting his eyes.

"What were you staring at?"

"Ah, Devin. I was... Thinking about you."

Devin's expression didn't change.

"Right... sure you were."

"Can't get anything past you... Just a not-so-bad-looking guy, that's all."

"You could shorten that to hot, you know."

Satisfied, Devin stepped back, clutching the glasses.

"Anyway, should I start getting the wedding invitations ready?"

Despite himself, Theo couldn't help but smile. He had to counteract it by slapping Devin's shoulder.

"Ow."

"Deserved. As usual."

Their tones were light, devoid of any actual ill-will.

They soon made it back to the table.

The moment they reached it, though, Devin put his phone to his ear with haste. His expression turned sour.

"Yeah? Ah. I'm sorry. Of course. I'll be right there."

Theo tapped the glass, uncomfortably glancing off to the side.

"Absolutely."

Putting it back, he eased his drink toward Theo.

"Uh, so... lucky you. You get an extra glass."

"It's okay."

"I don't think I can go into detail. But it seems like a bit of a personal crisis. I'm gonna have to go be emotional support."

"I get it. You're a good friend."

A pause.

"Don't forget yourself, Theo."

He caught a glimpse of a figure sliding by the edge of his peripheral vision.

When the person's movements suddenly ceased, intrigue drew his eyes to them. It was him. Standing under the orange glow of the lamp directly above him was the man Theo spotted earlier.

Such sharp and distinct features. He looked even more angelic up close. Or maybe the alcohol was starting to take effect. He had been drinking and sipping on the beer for a while.

His gaze shifted between the glasses and Theo, who probably wasn't looking too good standing alone with them.

"Hello there."

God? Is that you?

"I don't suppose I could have a taste of that untouched beer?"

Or the more likely option, Satan, considering the things that voice made Theo feel. Was it even possible for a man to have such a deep but silky one? You'd think it'd at least be a little coarse at that pitch.

"Interesting move... But I guess buying me one wouldn't make much sense. Yeah, you can have it if you want..." As Theo kept sipping his beer, the man leaned on the table in front of him, picking up what he had so graciously been offered.

He was speaking. Theo understood that much. Words were coming out of his mouth.

But... he wasn't paying a single bit of attention. All he heard was a tone so sweet, it sounded like a lullaby. That wasn't exactly helping him focus. The glass was getting emptier and emptier.

His eyes glazed over, settling on a minute splotch of black peeking out from under his rolled-up sleeve. A tattoo?

He noticed the man's arm move forward, urging him on.

"You can look."

Theo reached for the black fabric and gently pushed it up with his fingers, revealing more inked lines etched into his skin and up along his bicep.

"Feathers?"

"It's a bird, yeah."

"Ah, cool..." Theo absentmindedly played with the rim of the other man's sleeve with his thumb.

"Just the head of one. But you'd have to get me out of my shirt to see that."

"Hah... Right. Wait, huh?"

His momentary trance evaporated in an instant. He retracted his arm, finding it awfully hard to look him in the eyes all of a sudden. He had been too lulled in by the guy's voice and the little buzz the beer was giving him.

"Uh, hold on..." Damn did he wish more than ever that he was capable of dealing with this kind of situation in a level-headed manner.

At the very least, his companion looked to be somewhat amused.

Theo wasn't sure whether that was the reaction he wanted people to have, but at least he wasn't thrown off.

"Cute..."

"I-I'm not ..."

"I'll need that number of yours."

His smile stretched even further when Theo tensed up. Did he enjoy messing with someone so easily flustered?

"I'll... need a name first."

"Marco."

Watchful eyes studied every little movement Theo made, as he dipped his hand in his pocket and brought out his phone. After creating a new contact, he handed it over to him.

"I'm impressed. Or... surprised. Giving your phone to a stranger requires some courage."

Oh, that felt weirdly good.

"I try to believe the best in others... when I can." A certain brother came to mind.

"Admirable."

His eyes narrowed inquisitively on Theo before he turned his attention back to the screen glaring up at him.

After typing the numbers in, he gave Theo his phone back. Slowly. It took a minute before only Theo's hand was on it.

"I'll contact you later."

Theo slid it back into his pocket and stepped away from the table. As much as he appreciated the initiative Marco had taken, exhaustion was starting to creep in. He needed time to calm down by himself.

"I'll be waiting. Theo."

"How ..."

"At the top of the contact list."

"Mhm, of course." He watched Marco as the distance between them increased. A soft smile spread on his lips and remained until the man was completely out of sight.

As Theo pushed the door open, he was met with a rush of cold air. The quiet outside was like a wake-up call, bringing him back to reality. What kind of spell had he been under in there?

At the same time, all this street did was remind him of what he was going back to.

The only thing he could think to do was pull that electronic device right back out. And to be fair, that temptation was already far greater than his need for peace and calm.

Just a few quick messages, that would be all.

Chapter 2

The bustling city street was filled with energy. The air, a scent of coffee, mingled with the faint exhaust from passing cars. The honking horns, distant sirens, and chattering pedestrians created a constant, lively hum.

The pavement below him was solid but slightly uneven, worn smooth by countless footsteps. As Theo walked, he caught glimpses of storefronts, street signs, and the impressive skyscraper in the distance, its glass facade gleaming in the sunlight.

He had only planned to text Marco and get to know him better before taking it any further. And yet, somehow, he was on his way to meet him only a few days after their first-ever conversation.

He shuddered as someone's hand settled on his shoulder. When he turned to see who it was, an older woman with graying, shoulder-length hair met his cautious gaze. Letting go of his shoulder, she kept walking, encouraging Theo to keep up with her pace. He did as much, letting out a sigh of relief.

"What are you doing in the city?"

"I'm just dropping by to meet with Sylas."

He flinched at his mother's words.

"Oh. That's nice."

Audrey's eyes narrowed, but she kept quiet. As they continued down the busy street, a spark of tension hung in the air.

Theo had to break the silence himself.

"I'm, uh... Meeting up with someone, too."

"Devin?"

"...No."

She didn't respond and instead wrapped a firm hand around his.

That was always her way of hugging or showing support. Theo never really wondered why she didn't do it 'properly.' To him, it made sense. She had been like that since the beginning, reserved and cautious.

"I have to turn at the next corner."

"Have fun." The hint of a smile tugged at her lips as she retracted her hand.

He gave her a quick nod, then picked up the pace.

With a final lingering look back, he rounded the nearest street corner.

All around Theo, throngs of people pressed past each other, hurrying to get themselves and their relatives through the ticket gates.

One individual scooted into the main line, his eyes locked on Theo. It took him a second to realize who it was.

Others were moving up behind him, but he still beckoned with his hand for Theo to join him.

Theo's stomach tightened as he looked between Marco and the rest of the line. Wouldn't he be skipping them? But that should be allowed since they're supposed to go in together, right?

... and every other imaginable question.

Marco tried to extend his arm as far as possible, mouthing something Theo couldn't interpret.

"Theo."

In the end, the only thing that actually got him to move was a louder version of the voice that pulled him in at the bar.

He squeezed himself into the queue with hesitant steps, finding comfort in the large form standing beside him.

It certainly wasn't helping that the people behind him were scrunching their noses and glaring at them.

Hiding wasn't possible, was it?

"Were you about to run away?" Marco laughed.

"Uh, maybe. I just don't want to bother ..."

They're still staring.

"... Anyone"

"Hey, at least you're not bothering me." That was only somewhat calming. He had no reason to be, so that was purely to make Theo relax.

"That's... good."

"So, who was the woman you were talking to?"

"You saw... Well, that was my mother. She doesn't actually live here, though. Said something about visiting my brother, Silas."

Marco's brow arched when he noticed how Theo recoiled at the name.

"Not a fan of him?"

"That's putting it mildly. I mean, he even has to live in the same city as me? Really? Right at ..." He almost stopped himself, but Silas's address slipped out.

"No need to worry. I'll help keep your mind off him. Just focus on me."

How could Theo say no to that?

The zoo was large and expansive. Its walkways were smooth and winding, leading visitors through enclosures and exhibits. The sound of chirping birds and distant roars created a lively atmosphere.

They felt the sun's warmth on their skin as they strolled through the landscaped areas and well-maintained gardens.

The first exhibits they visited were inhabited by various different exotic bird species.

Marco's face lit up at the colorful sight.

Casting a quick glance at his arm, Theo was reminded of the tattoo.

"So, birds are a big deal to you?"

"Well, I'm mostly a fan of corvids. But yeah, love 'em."

"That kind of makes me wonder what you usually do. Like, fun or work."

"Ah, a classic question."

Theo sensed a hint of disdain in his tone.

"I mostly just try to survive at my office job and work out. Sometimes, I dare venture out into the nightlife. As you saw."

For some reason, Theo expected this guy to be doing more... daring things? He had no idea what that would even be, but still.

"Pretty much the same for me. Except for the working out part. And the office part. Uh, anyway, I just work at a gas station. But I do like to travel sometimes. When the money is there." So, not very often.

"I'd love to travel too, but I don't have much time for it."

Theo wanted to question him further, but Marco was already headed for the nearest enclosure.

They walked past a multitude of different animals. Stopping mainly at the crocodiles, other smaller reptiles, and wolves.

By the time they reached the tiger exhibit, their conversation had turned to everything involving carnivores and that one wolf that practically stared them down.

"Ruthless, aren't they?"

"I guess... but I like them. Despite their size. I got one of the smaller ones at home."

"You have a cat?"

"Ever since I first moved out, yeah." Theo's eyes drifted to the other end of the park they were currently in, landing on a red-brown sheen coming from a few flowing locks.

Devin.

He had to go see him.

Marco was about to speak up but stopped himself.

"I-I'm sorry. I might have to cut today short."

"Oh... that's alright." He carefully eyed the person Theo had been gazing at.

"We'll figure out a new time as soon as possible."

"Great." Marco slid his hand down Theo's arm, making his face flush.

"Oh, uh, yeah. Bye."

Slipping out of his loose grip, Theo headed after his friend.

"Devin! What's up? I didn't expect to see you here." Of course he did; he mentioned wanting to go. Formalities.

Devin stepped back in surprise.

"I should be saying that. Who—"

In his eagerness, he cut Devin off.

"Hope all went well with your friend."

"It was fine. You know how those things are. It's usually not that black and white..." He glanced past Theo's shoulder.

Theo turned his head just as Marco disappeared from view.

"I'd rather you tell me what's going on with that guy."

"Oh, Marco? Yeah, he's... nice."

"Ooh." Devin's lips curled up.

"Didn't you just ditch him for me?"

"Yeah, but... You probably had to deal with some tough feelings. You need the company more. If my company is worth much, that is."

Devin listened intently, furrowing his brows by the end.

"Always."

A house, huh? That was the first time he had met someone around his age who didn't have an apartment, especially in and around the city.

Even though it had been a while since they last saw each other, Theo was still fiddling with his shirt sleeves, glancing both left and right as if someone was going to sneak up on him.

"I got work pretty early after finishing school. And I've just been saving up since then."

"Impressive..."

Marco stepped back, standing just behind his door frame.

"Don't look so nervous; we're not going there right away. Unless you want to." Looking back over his shoulder, Marco disappeared into the dark, his footsteps receding into the distance.

Theo gulped. At least now he knew they were on the same page.

The inside felt modern, with cold, smooth marble flooring that reflected the soft ambient light from the pendant lamps.

His living room was certainly a spectacle. The large windows let in natural light, casting warm, inviting shadows on the velvet furniture.

Velvet, huh?

Admittedly, he was just trying to distract himself. It was growing a bit quiet.

"I know I said we weren't. But, looking at you standing there so innocently, I..."

Marco's voice snapped him back to reality. Who were they kidding?

"... Where's the bedroom?" A tinge of pride was attached to those words.

The other man's eyes widened at that.

"Well then... right this way."

Under him lay the softest sheets he ever had the pleasure to touch. He could fall into the depths of Marco's king bed and disappear forever.

But that would mean having to ignore the man towering above him.

"Just relax. I'll take care of everything."

As his black shirt was thrown to the side, Theo finally saw the rest of the bird's head. The artist must have spent quite a while making it. The details were so finely done he shuddered to think what it might have cost.

Nothing left Theo's lips. He just watched Marco's half-naked body as he took something out of the nightstand.

He traced the ink with his finger, taking in a deep breath to calm himself. Their eyes connected for a moment. Marco was already ripping a tiny packet open with his teeth.

Straight to the point.

"Oh..."

Shedding them both of their clothes, Marco slicked his rubber-covered cock in lube.

His hands then ever so gently traveled across Theo's thighs. And with a light but steady grip, he pulled him closer.

As Marco buried himself deep inside Theo, one thought remained. But only for a moment before vanishing with a sudden jolt of pleasure. One that made his mind go blank and kept it there for the rest of the night.

How was he so slow and caring but controlling at the same time? Something wasn't matching in his head—a disharmony of sorts.

"I want you. All to myself."

Chapter 3

"What did I do this time, Briar?"

He had been acting distant since Theo came home from Marco's place and was first now climbing onto his lap. A spot he usually ended up in by the end of the day.

Of course, he got no answer. But he had a pretty good guess.

"Your little nose is too powerful. Don't worry, though; he's a nice guy."

A familiar knocking came from the entrance hall. Someone was at the door.

Any other knock normally wouldn't paralyze him, but there he was, leaning against the couch, refusing to get up.

With a growl, Briar jumped off and left through the living room door, stalking down the hallway.

He was reminded of when he was younger, when Silas would practically break down the door after finding out some unfortunate thing Theo had kept from the family or the few occasions he let something slip to the neighbors.

After his little 'visit', it would take hours every day for at least a week to get Theo to speak to the rest of the family—or even join them for dinner.

Briar had no idea. He was adopted when Theo moved out, after all. To him, this could just as easily be Devin.

"Theodore."

It didn't necessarily sound aggressive yet. But Silas's voice was still loud. How did he not care even the slightest about annoying the neighbors?

Theo slipped off the couch and managed to get himself out into the hallway, where Briar followed him closely.

With shaky hands, Theo unlocked the door and turned the handle.

Before he could get a good look at his visitor, the door slammed open and hit the wall. He shuddered, nearly jumping back as his breath caught in his throat.

Briar backed away, its tail puffed up.

"Took you long enough."

Theo didn't know where to look, and it certainly wasn't going to be Silas's face. It felt like the walls of the small space were closing in on him.

"What? So repressed you can't even respond to me anymore?"

His smile was... disconcerting, to say the least.

"Why are you here?"

Silas closed the door behind himself.

"Because it's over. We both knew that, though, didn't we? We were never a real fucking family to begin with. But it's time I said it straight to your face."

Theo couldn't keep his eyes away from him anymore. All that stared back at him were two soulless, empty pupils.

Briar was weaving around their legs, brushing his body against them, to try and mitigate the situation.

"I-I'm sorry you feel that way." A reactionary response. He was way too shaky to come up with anything else.

"You—"

Once the cat finally caught Silas's attention, his mood tempered for a second.

An unbearably long second, where none of them spoke.

And yet, if only it hadn't stopped.

Theo barely had time to register the clenched fist before it connected with his jaw. His lip got caught between his teeth, tearing the tender skin. Blood seeped into his mouth, its metallic taste mingling with the sharp sting of the split lip.

Staggering backward, he pressed a hand against his lower face, trying to stem the bleeding. From the corner of his eye, he noticed Briar launching himself at Silas, claws extended and teeth bared. He swiftly latched onto his leg, biting down hard.

"Fuck."

That irritated look on his face. No...

"Wait—"

The instant Silas' shoe hit Briar's small body, Theo dropped to the floor beside him.

"Don't bother contacting me. Ever." He left the apartment with a loud slam of the door.

"Briar..." His fingers combed through the shuddering cat's fur, petting the impacted area. He maintained eye contact, making sure he understood he was safe.

Theo had betrayed himself once again. He didn't even try to fight back. And after Briar tried his best to help him as well.

A soft meow left the animal as its tail wrapped around its body.

Theo could feel Briar's heartbeat slow down under his hand, its front leg stretching across Theo's forearm.

"There's my boy."

For a moment, the tiniest smile spread across his lips.

He was, regrettably, used to Silas's aggression. But this was something else. Something... more permanent.

At the same time, a nagging feeling gnawed at him. There was no way this could have gone unprompted.

Either way, all that kept ringing in his head was that he no longer had a brother.

But, did he ever?

The door swung open.

"Hey... Theo." Devin's eyes narrowed when they reached his mouth.

"Wow, okay. I didn't think he left a mark. That's pretty messed up."

Theo stepped inside and locked the door.

"Yeah..."

They walked past white wall after white wall. Theo's mind was all a blur.

"Want something to drink?"

"I could use some coffee." He was having trouble sleeping recently. Not that caffeine was going to help.

"Alright, I'll make some and meet you in the living room."

Theo sat down, placing his phone on the table with the coffee mug.

Theo tugged at the rim of his sleeves, watching it with glazed eyes.

"You're being a bit dismissive. Which makes me wonder... How did you feel about Silas at that moment?"

"Huh? Well, I just... I'm mad."

Devin's eyes lit up.

"Sorry, I was mad. That I didn't do anything."

... His face fell again.

"No, Theo. Him. Weren't you mad at him?"

"Oh... Right. Yeah, of course."

Devin's eyebrows drew together, and he stayed quiet, forcing Theo to continue.

"I feel like you're trying to psychoanalyze me. Stop that."

Seeing Theo timidly pick up his coffee mug and put it to his lips, Devin leaned back, breaking their eye contact momentarily.

"I wish I was better at being there for you. Silently. I know that's probably what you need..."

Theo smiled. He removed the cup from his mouth and warmed his hands on it.

"It's okay. I know you're just trying to help."

Devin returned it.

"I want to know why you're being so held back, though. Why can't you just hate him?"

"Anyone looking in would think I'm crazy for not having cut him off already. But I've had good times. Good memories. He wasn't always bad. I loved him as a brother. Sometimes..."

"But Theo... That's just an abusive relationship, no?"

"You're right, but... it still hurts to lose him, even though I should probably be happy."

"I get it. It's hard if it's someone you've known for a long time."

Devin paused.

"I still feel like you're too forgiving."

Theo stared back down at the cup in his hands. Warily, he took another sip.

"Mmh..."

"What about Audrey? Are you going to tell her?"

"Not... yet."

With a nod, Devin picked up his own cup right as Theo had to place his back down. A sharp glow lit up the phone's screen.

It was a text from Marco.

He responded, then put it away in his pocket.

Devin arched a brow.

"Marco. The guy you saw me with at the zoo."

"So it's getting serious, huh?"

"Uhm... maybe. I don't know." Theo's face felt a little hot. It didn't help that a wave of mental images were pressing their way to the forefront of his mind.

"I won't press you on it. Unless you want me to."

"Oh, absolutely not. We've talked enough about me. I just want to relax."

"Want to play something? Watch something?"

"Yes, please. I don't want to think about any of this anymore."

"That can be arranged."

Theo could always rely on him. That, he never doubted.

Standing before a large, mostly glass-stained building stood Marco, wearing an unexpectedly white shirt.

He waved Theo over. But his face dropped when he got what he wanted.

"What happened to you?"

He really didn't need to relive that right now.

"Oh, I just got into a little skirmish with Silas. If you remember who that is. Please don't worry about it."

"But…"

"I already talked to my friend Devin. I'm alright."

Marco's brows furrowed as he glanced off to the side. His body tensed up; it really looked like he wanted to say something. But instead, he pushed the door to the cinema open.

"Okay. Let's just enjoy the movie, then."

After making it through the lobby and a few dark corridors, they got to the entrance to the auditorium. The number above it shone, matching what they had been told by the staff.

Before them stretched row upon row of seats. The giant screen filled the room with a soft, bluish glow. Commercials played, illuminating the outlines of every seat and the few early arrivals who had already settled in.

Marco's eyes locked on someone further up the stairs on the side.

Though he didn't know Marco's relation to the person, Theo also recognized him. He'd seen the man a few times before at the cinema. He worked here.

Hurrying to their seats before the lights dimmed, they nestled into them and against each other. However, Theo's attention kept slipping from the screen to the silhouette previously at the top of the stairs.

"Do you know that guy?" Theo's voice lowered to a whisper.

"Just an old acquaintance of mine." So did Marco's.

"Ah, that's all?"

"…Yes. Look, it's starting."

As always, he wanted to ask so many questions. However, all he did was lean against Marco's shoulder, trying to comfort himself and win some favor back. Noticing the faint smile spreading across the man's face, he knew he had succeeded.

Silence swept over the dark room as the movie took over the next few hours of their date.

Back down in the main lobby, the two were on their way to the main doors, shoulders as close as ever.

The story hadn't struck much of a cord with them. Halfway through, they were more eager to get closer to one another in the dark than to pay any attention to what they were actually there for.

It took them a second to realize that the rain was pouring heavily when they got outside.

A quick glance at each other was all it took for them to rush back inside. With labored breaths, they leaned against the nearest wall.

It went quiet as Theo's gaze drifted downward. The white fabric covering Marco's body clung to his skin. It was... very transparent.

He had to stand a little differently once his blood decided to gather in a very inconvenient area.

"I guess we gotta wait it out." First now did Marco notice where all of Theo's attention was going.

"Or... Would you rather do something else?"

"I mean... It would be pretty boring just to wait, right?"

Marco's grin spread further as he wrapped his hand around Theo's arm, pulling him back into the dark corridors. This time, the ones leading to the bathroom.

Theo's back hit the wall as Marco locked the stall door behind himself.

But... something was still nagging at him. His uncertainty about doing this in public made focusing on anything but the man in front of him easier.

As he got closer, Theo placed his hands gently on his shoulders.

"I want to know what's going on with that person from earlier."

Marco's lip twitched as a rough hand made its way down Theo's stomach, lingering dangerously close to his crotch.

"You're asking too many questions."

Once he came into contact with Theo's clothed cock, his grip tightened around its visible shape.

"W-Wait."

Theo inhaled sharply.

"Already hard, huh?" Sliding his hand inside, Marco closed it around Theo, making him gasp.

"Marco..."

Theo covered his mouth to quiet the moans that so desperately wanted to escape.

"Shh..."

His fingers brushed over the split lip's indent, making him freeze. His hand landed on Marco's chest, trying to get as far away from the memories as possible.

"I..."

A warm sensation spread throughout his body as Marco kept pumping his hand on Theo's cock.

He grasped the man's wet shirt, crinkling it under his shaky fingers, which soon dug into Marco's skin. The heated sound he got in response made his face flare up.

That's right. His voice. As siren-like as always. Lulling Theo into another world.

He could feel the end getting near. His body trembled. His mind went blank. His back slammed hard against the wall. And before he knew it, it was all over.

Chapter 4

Theo couldn't get the mysterious man out of his head. And after yesterday, it was time he took some initiative for once.

Briar stood beside him in the hallway, his tiny head rubbing against Theo's calf.

"This is a good decision, right?"

Noticing his owner was speaking to him, Briar lifted his head and let out a low, growling meow.

"You're so wise." He unlocked the front door, making the dark creature below him step back and let out another meow.

"I'll be back later. I've given you plenty of food and toys to play with, so no complaining."

Its yellow eyes gleamed at him. No sound came from Briar this time.

Why did it feel like he was worried about Theo? He had been a bit extra clingy ever since the incident with Silas.

"Love you."

The door clicked shut.

Theo surveyed every area of the lobby, keeping an eye out for anyone wearing staff colors.

He found a few, but it took a moment before the guy arrived. Theo took a deep breath.

Once he was ready, he trotted right up to him.

"Uhm. You, uh..."

His head turned slightly, confused but intrigued.

"Hello? Do you need help with anything?"

The air this man exuded was quite striking. Not to mention, he was conventionally attractive. His ruffled, dark-brown hair easily drew Theo's attention, and the facial hair was a nice touch, too.

"Do you know someone named... Marco?"

The polite staff smile Theo had found comfort in immediately vanished from the man's face.

"How do you know about him?"

"We're... friends? Or, uh, something similar..."

"Oh."

"I was here with him yesterday. He saw you, and, well, he seemed pretty interested. Or, at least, he was staring a lot. When I asked him about you, he was very dismissive."

Luca didn't respond; his expression was unreadable.

"So, uh... I just got curious."

"Sorry. I can't discuss this right now. You can tell me your number, though, and I'll get back to you later."

Something about the professional tone made Theo lower his guard. He easily handed those numbers out verbally.

"Great. If you don't have any plans for the next few days, I'll figure something out."

"Ah, sure."

"I'll get back to work then. See you."

A lingering look and he was gone once again.

What was Theo supposed to feel? Even he had no idea.

The man's texts were very brief and to the point.

Before Theo knew it, he was sitting on a couch by the wall of the same bar he always visited with Devin. The place where he first met Marco.

He considered getting a drink while waiting, but instead, he ended up getting more sweat on his phone as he held it tightly in his hands.

He didn't have to worry about it for long as a familiar figure soon entered, slamming the door closed with haste. The noise made him jump, his eyes landing on the man wearing a brown aviator jacket.

His gaze swept over the bar counter, but he found nothing.

Theo considered speaking up but couldn't get himself to do it. The new impression he was getting of the guy made it hard to know how to react.

When he finally noticed Theo, he gave him a quick nod. And as he got closer, Theo could feel his body sink into the couch.

"What drink do you want? I'll pay."

"Oh, I couldn't. You don't have to do that."

The man's eyes narrowed.

"Huh... I see what's happening here." He was mostly muttering to himself, but it wasn't as if Theo couldn't hear him. His hand tightened around the phone.

"Let's just talk."

A smile flashed across the stranger's face.

"Tell me what you want."

Theo's eyebrows drew together, which actually seemed to please him, dragging his smile out further.

"...Buy me whatever you're getting."

Satisfied, he turned and headed to the counter.

This was way too different from the polite guy he expected to meet here. He was working the other time, though.

When he returned and sat on the couch opposite Theo, two small glasses were placed on the table. Putting his phone away, Theo took a tentative sip of the one closest to him. The taste of alcohol hit him immediately; it was hard liquor.

"Whiskey?"

"If you wanted something else, you could have said so."

"Nnh."

"It's Luca, by the way."

"Theo."

"So, about that guy... He..." Luca dragged every word out, finding it hard to continue. He even stopped to take a drink from his glass. His index finger tapped repeatedly against it.

"Ugh..."

Behind him, a certain someone entered the bar. Theo's face lit up, and so did Luca's. He had been saved from following himself up.

"What is it?"

"Ah... A friend."

Devin waved at him but didn't approach them until Theo beckoned him over.

"Interesting. Now you're hanging out with another hot guy. Since when did you get so popular?" Devin chuckled.

Holding the glass close to his face, Theo somehow thought it was even remotely large enough to hide him.

"Oh? Well, you don't look so bad yourself." Luca leaned back.

"I would blush if I was... into anyone. It's appreciated, though."

"Ah, damn. A shame. But I shouldn't say that, should I? How often do you get that?"

Something clicked for Devin. He even sat down on the couch next to Luca.

"Don't even get me started. As if your life isn't worth anything if you don't plan to spend it grotesquely combined with someone else's."

"Of course. That's for each person to decide for themselves."

Theo tugged at his own sleeves.

"Guys? I'm sorry to interrupt. It's just... we didn't get to finish ..."

Luca's gaze landed on him.

"Hmm?"

"N-Nevermind."

His hazy expression morphed into a glare. Much easier to interpret, but not exactly ideal.

"Would you be worried about something as simple as knocking a glass off the table? Since it'll slightly inconvenience someone?"

Theo stared silently at him, watching as Luca leaned across the table and picked up his glass. He didn't like where this was going. Luca's glare was soon replaced by a wide grin that grew as the glass slowly slid down his fingers. He was threatening to drop it.

"No, don't."

Nothing.

"Please?"

His plea seemed to do something to Luca. The hand shook a little.

That was the opposite of what Theo wanted.

As a last resort, Theo similarly leaned over the table to try and catch it. But... his actions were in vain.

His elbow connected with the glass beside him, and down went his own drink. Onto the floor—in pieces.

To Theo's surprise, Devin hadn't interfered with them, leaving Theo increasingly panicked and unsure what to think.

A staff member heard the commotion and was ready with tools to help clean up the mess.

"I-I'm so sorry. I didn't mean to."

Luca drank the rest of the whiskey with a much tighter grip, looking more than pleased with his actions.

"No, no, it's alright. It happens... far too often here anyway." With a smile, they removed everything staining the floor. Their calm demeanor made Theo go quiet.

Once the three were alone again, Theo noted the fact that his friend wasn't looking to share any glances with him.

However, Luca's gaze was intense. And, in a serious tone, he uttered a set of words that Theo wouldn't soon forget.

"This can't keep going. Or he'll eat you up."

They might not have cared, but another employee could have been genuinely annoyed.

Everything that happened that day was replaying in Theo's head. He had no hope of paying attention to the man beside him.

"You've been a bit distracted today, Theo. Are you okay?"

"I'm sorry."

"That's not an answer." Marco laughed.

He really wasn't there. It didn't even register for him to return the gesture with at least a smile.

"There's... just a lot going on right now."

"You know, you can always talk to me about it."

Audrey. That's who he needed to talk to. How could he forget?

He'd thank Marco for the reminder but couldn't delay his much-needed conversation with Audrey. After the day at the bar, he felt renewed courage. Somehow. That Luca guy ...

"I need to go visit Audrey."

A hint of recognition flashed across Marco's face. Not confusion.

"Uh, my mom."

"Right, of course."

His smile would've been a lot less eerie if it made any sense for it to be there.

"I'll see you soon, right?"

"Sure. We'll plan something."

Theo was struck by how much easier it was to cut it off this time.

It may have helped that Marco was okay with it. Uncomfortably so.

Theo gave him one last look before heading back to the parking lot.

As the gray car came into view, Theo put his phone to his ear. Audrey's number was on the line, but no one was picking up.

She shouldn't be busy today, as far as he knew.

As he climbed into his car, determined to see her, a deep, hollow pit formed in his stomach.

Chapter 5

No wind stirred the leaves of the trees surrounding the house. No neighbors tended to their gardens. Strangest of all, her car wasn't there.

Peering through the windows as he passed, he saw no signs of activity inside.

He hesitated, not sure he wanted the answer knocking on the door would provide.

And sure enough, nothing.

He looked through the glass, scouring the house's interior as if she would magically appear the second time.

Growing increasingly restless, he let out a deep sigh, and his phone was again back by his ear.

"Hey, Devin. Are you free? I was wondering if I could come over."

There was no immediate answer. Instead, another voice could be heard in the background. One that didn't match any of the people he knew Devin hung out with. Yet he still recognized it.

"Sure, man. As long as you're okay with Luca being there."

"Oh. Uh, yeah, that's fine."

They must have kept in contact. After Luca's abrupt dismissal at the bar, this could be another chance to get some answers.

"Get over here then." It was almost possible to hear the smile in his voice. That already made Theo feel a lot less tense.

"Hey. You sounded a bit distressed. Do you want to talk about it, or should we just do something fun?" Devin stood in the doorway, inviting him inside.

Theo was about to answer but stopped himself after Luca came into view.

"Sorry, uh, one second."

He pushed past Devin, getting face-to-face with his guest.

"Hey, Luca."

"Mmh?"

"Could you... explain yourself already?"

His nose scrunched up in amusement.

"Ah, capable of at least some confrontation, are we? But what exactly do you want me to explain?"

"Everything. I mean, Marco."

"Just stay away from him."

Not exactly an answer. And something Theo couldn't possibly do that easily.

Devin was once again staying quiet.

"Unhelpful."

Luca's lips stretched out into a smile.

"What's unhelpful is your trust in him."

Still with the vagueness. It was all starting to get to Theo. That tense feeling from earlier returned in full force.

With his eyes locked on Luca, he spoke into the device his hand was getting very familiar with recently.

"Marco? ... Yeah. As soon as you can. My place."

Luca's face dropped.

The call ended immediately after that.

"Don't."

"Watch me."

Out Theo went, slamming the door behind him. It didn't feel good leaving Devin like that. But he was of no mind to turn back now.

At home, with little time to reflect, Theo's first thought was to apologize, as usual. However, his texts with Devin soon turned into a new plan to meet up.

Knocking came from the door, quite different from the one that still haunted him and threatened his sleep every night—a true nightmare.

Marco was quick. He expected a bit more time to himself.

Nonetheless, that meant he could finally bury those thoughts for now.

Opening the door for his late-night visitor, he was met with quite the disheveled sight. He clearly didn't waste time.

Just what Theo needed.

"Couldn't wait to see me again either? I knew your love was as stro—"

Cutting Marco off with his mouth, Theo deftly locked the door before shoving him against it.

Marco's eyes widened initially, but he closed them once Theo was in his hands.

This time, what was usually a natural part of Theo's encounters irked him. However, he didn't have it in him to do anything about it—not in the throes of desire and a need for escape.

One thing that stayed on his mind, however, was how Marco got here.

He never told him his address.

Theo was back in the old bar yet again after a much-needed break.

He'd like to think so, at least. Sitting in the dark corner, his foot tapped impatiently at the floor.

Devin wasn't here yet. He was always so punctual.

The extra minutes were bleeding into hours.

A quiet hum came from his pocket.

Taking the source out, Theo saw the last name he expected.

"Hey. Do you know if Devin is busy or something? He hasn't been returning my calls, messages, or anything."

That was the very last thing Theo wanted to hear.

"No... No, I don't know. We were meant to meet today, but..."

Luca didn't respond at first, and at that moment, Theo's eyes landed on an oddly familiar person sitting in the far corner of the room. Someone was just getting up from the couch in front of him.

"Are you okay, Theo?"

"Marco...?"

"Huh?"

"I think I see him. He was talking to someone."

"I'm begging you. You need to be direct with him. As soon as possible."

"... What if I talked to him now?"

"Wait. Where are you? I'll be there."

"The bar."

"Don't do anything until you see me."

Theo felt conflicted, but the genuine concern in Luca's voice was swaying him.

"Fine. But hurry."

Time crawled by as he continued to wait for him. And for some reason, all Marco did the entire time was look at his phone. He hadn't looked up once since the other guy left.

That, however, changed in a split second when another man stormed in through the main entrance. His eyes widened, and the distraction was gone.

Luca spotted the two in their separate corners, beckoned Theo to him with his hand, then marched over to where Marco was sitting.

Theo followed him, nearly bumping into a few chairs along the way.

Once they got there, Marco stood up—desperate to even the power balance between them.

In the presence of those two, his so-called vigor was quick to dissipate. If they weren't intimidating enough on their own, this sudden tension was enough to make Theo shudder.

"Luca... You know, I've missed you quite a lot."

"Mhm. Sure, you have. Why don't you tell your 'good friend' here what you've been up to? I'd also really like to know myself."

"As unfriendly as ever. What, pray tell, could you be talking about?"

"Well, Theo? Answer him."

He almost forgot he was even there. The sudden attention on him made his hands shake, as they so often did.

"Uh—"

"Don't listen to him. You believe in me, don't you?"

"Stop. Just... tell me. Do you know anything about Devin? My mother? Silas? Did you... do something?"

Marco's eyes darted between Luca's intense gaze and the resigned Theo.

"Okay. Alright. I understand. How can you trust or love me if I'm not being honest with you? Maybe you'll even understand that I did it for you. For us."

The underlying unease he had felt with Marco recently was finally showing itself. No more veils. It made Theo shudder.

But Luca? He looked right at home.

"I talked to your brother. Told him to cut you off. Completely. Whatever else happened, I wouldn't know. Though, with the way he acted, I could only imagine."

Theo was stunned, unable to react. Even as Marco's hand gently cradled his cheek, his thumb tracing Theo's lower lip.

Luca couldn't bear to watch any longer. He grabbed Marco by the forearm, pushing him back.

"What else, asshole?"

He only spared Luca a single glance, keeping his eyes on his 'beloved.'

"He was bad for you anyway. It was a quick, direct way for you to be done with him. But of course... Hanging out with your mother would also take away from our time. So I dealt with her. Little threats go a long way."

"'Little', huh? I doubt that." Luca cut in, knowing Theo couldn't respond at the moment.

"Shut it," Marco snapped. "You mentioned Devin as well? Yeah, you're too close to someone considered a friend. So... I think you get it."

Theo didn't know how he'd ever be able to comment on that.

"My... My address... How?"

"I kept in contact with Silas afterward. He's a bit crazy, but I got some good information from him."

That's when Theo finally snapped back, on high alert.

"Yeah? Crazy? What about you? Did you hear anything you just said?"

Marco looked quite taken aback. As if Theo's reaction wasn't justifiable.

"But... You don't need those people, Theo."

"This is too much..."

Without looking back, Theo sprinted out of the building, knocking over a chair on his way out.

Tears formed in the corners of his eyes, quickly whisked away by the fresh air as he stepped outside. He needed to get away. There was no way he was ever opening those doors again.

Speaking of, he heard them swing open in the distance but paid it no mind.

According to his frazzled mind, the city's inner park was the best spot to think. It wasn't too large, but it tended to be quiet this late in the evening.

Soft, warm lights from nearby lampposts and surrounding buildings cast a golden glow, contrasting the moon's otherwise cold blue light.

The green leaves rustling in the wind above him, the distinct chirping of nocturnal birds, and even the flowing fountain in the middle of the park did nothing to soothe him.

His throat felt dry.

Sitting on one of the roughed-up, brown benches, Theo stared lifelessly at the spring water.

Footsteps drowned out the chirping, but Theo didn't react. The person said nothing. They just came closer and closer until the bench creaked beneath him.

"Are some of those sounds coming from owls...?" He didn't look away from the fountain.

"Could be. I've never listened to birds out here this late. I'm usually a few drinks down." A warm laugh, but a cautious one.

"Can I stay at your place tonight?"

The bench creaked again as the other man shifted beside him.

"I... Sure. Why—"

As Theo put a hand to his own ear, Luca went quiet.

"I don't know if you expected anything else, but it's over, Marco. Stay away from me."

Hanging up, he turned to face Luca. He was smiling, likely pleased by the reference to his own words.

"I don't feel safe at my apartment right now. So..."

The smile didn't last long.

"Right. Let's go. Is there anything you need to get from your place, though?"

Briar.

"Wait, yes. I need to go get my cat first. And his food. His cage. Toys."

He wasn't even trying to hide his concern for that animal. It made Luca's lips curve up just a bit again.

"Oh no, am I first now learning you're some crazy cat person? Can I bail on this?"

"Fuck you."

"Ooh, there's the aggression I've been searching for."

With a quick glare Luca's way, Theo's up from the bench and raring to go.

He could figure out how to get this nightmare over with later. For now, hiding was his highest priority.

Chapter 6

Messages kept coming in. Filled with threats, guilt-tripping, and the occasional apology.

Of course, Theo didn't pick up the calls. He eventually had to shut the thing off.

"We're here. Just park along the sidewalk."

His apartment building stood just outside the most populated parts of the neighboring city. The area reminded Theo of the suburbs his mother lived in.

Doing as he had been told, he got out of the car and headed directly for the trunk.

Moments later, Luca joined him just as he was pulling the cage out.

"You can take him inside. I'll carry the rest." Luca flung a set of keys toward Theo, who barely caught them with his free hand.

"Second floor. My name's on the plaque."

Theo looked at the rattled cat, confused by all the sudden transportation, then back at Luca.

"Thank you."

Standing in a living room similar to his own, Theo already felt at home, and simplicity was a big factor in that. One thing he found curious, though, was the metal bar with two 'hooks' attached to the top of the doorframe leading to the bedroom.

"There's something I should probably tell you, Theo."

Everything had been set up for Briar. But he wasn't ready to start running around and getting comfortable just yet. He remained glued to Theo's leg. New places, new people. And after what happened with Silas, no wonder he wasn't too trusting.

"What is it?"

"I mostly agreed to let you stay because it would be better if we were two. But he still knows about this place. He has... For a long time."

Since Theo didn't respond right away, he had to cut in.

"All we can do is hope he doesn't find out we're here."

"I do remember how dismissive he was about you. And whatever was going on at the bar. I'm guessing you're never going to tell me what happened between you two?"

Luca sighed.

"No."

He walked past Theo and disappeared through the bedroom door.

Theo picked up Briar's cat bed and went in after him.

"All I'll say is... humans are easily manipulated."

Theo felt a lump forming in his throat as Luca sat down on the bed. He hadn't really accounted for this. Of course, he would only have one.

"I can just... go sleep on the couch."

"What kind of host would I be? I'll let you have the bed." Luca got up again. But before he could take another step, Theo stopped him.

"Wait... Stay here."

Theo was struggling to meet his gaze.

He just wanted the comfort of Luca's protection. Right?

Luca opened his mouth to respond, but nothing came out. Instead, he smiled and exhaled through his nose. Right.

As the sun's rays touched his skin, his immediate impulse was to find where it came from. The bedroom's single mirror was open. Potentially to let some morning air in. Luca must have done it before leaving, as he was nowhere to be found.

A peculiar sight rested on the windowsill.

Briar sat there, the limp body of a jackdaw hanging from its mouth. Grasped securely in its claws.

Exasperated, Theo hurried out of bed.

"Oh god."

His hand came close to the dead creature as it fell onto the wood, but he couldn't get himself to touch it.

"Luca? If you're there, could you maybe bring me a trash bag and some gloves?" He raised his voice, but not to the point of yelling.

Rummaging noises came from further away. Lucky.

Luca entered moments later, plastic in hand.

"I don't have any gloves. What did you need this for?"

Theo didn't need to say much; all he had to do was glance past the cat's proud face and at the lump below him.

"Ah."

With absolutely no shame, Luca grabbed the bird and shoved it into the bag.

"Jeez." Theo winced.

"Any plans for today?"

"Devin. I know it might be hopeless to try and find him at his house. You know, if he was threatened the same way as my mother. Whatever way that was. But... I don't know what else to do."

"Want me to come with you?"

"I'd feel safer if you did..."

"Let's hurry, then."

It took a few knocks. But eventually, and much to Theo's surprise, the door opened.

"Oh, hey. I didn't think you'd actually be here."

Devin's eyes were downcast, barely making eye contact with either of them.

"When I saw you through the window, I did consider not letting you in. But..." He paused, walking further back to make space for them.

They only stepped into the entrance, closing the door behind them. It wasn't locked.

"Good. This won't take long. I want to be left alone today."

Luca wasn't cutting in; he just stood by to let them talk.

"You don't have to explain yourself if it's too hard."

"It's fine. I don't want to keep it to myself. Plus, I like you too much."

They exchanged cautious smiles.

"It's just... I've never seen you this shaken up before." Theo had seen him messed up and vocal about it, not resigned like this.

"I always tell the people in my community to speak up, no matter what. I'd be a bad example."

Theo had to wonder when that would eventually become destructive.

"Then, tell me."

Devin let out a long, drawn-out sigh.

"Marco visited me. He was threatening me to stay away from you. While... making advances on me. I'm not going into detail. I'd rather die. He said he'd go further if I kept being your friend. That he'd do much... worse things."

Luca's lip twitched, which he quickly dulled by biting it.

There was nothing Theo could say that'd be good enough. He just stood there in shock before rushing to wrap his arms around his friend. Devin shuddered.

"I-I'm sorry." Theo jerked back a bit but was stopped when Devin held even tighter onto him.

"Don't be."

It wasn't often that he held onto him with such vigor. Their hugs were usually very brief.

"Disgusting creature." Luca's bitter words broke the silence.

"Theo... I want to escape this. Come with me to the next festival I'm going to. It's starting in a few days. You can come too, Luca."

"Of course. If that's what you want." Letting go, they stepped back, gauging each other's mood.

"Thank you. Please leave me alone for now. I'll meet you there. I need to take another shower..."

"How many times have you done that today?"

"At least two... Three."

"Please be careful, Devin."

"Yeah, I'll deal with that problem after I've gotten your boyfriend off of me; thank you."

That one felt like a verbal slap. Considering everything he was learning about Marco, it was getting harder to imagine he was ever into him. What a tricky thing.

"Ah... Uh, right, of course."

"We'll gladly see you at the festival. Hope you get some deserved time to yourself." Luca grabbed Theo by the arm and reeled him back out of the apartment.

"Thank you. Let's just forget about it all for a bit. Then, you can both do whatever you want." Devin closed the door for them, keeping eye contact with Theo until the click.

"I want to go talk to Marco. Like, right now."

"What did he just say, Theo?"

"Ugh, I know."

"Let's go home for now."

It was going to be a restless few days for Theo.

Theo felt the cool concrete floor underfoot as they navigated through the crowded aisles.

The dim lighting, punctuated by spotlights, highlighted the attendees' eclectic outfits and the striking merchandise on display.

It was almost impossible to count the number of harnesses and similar articles of clothing hanging in nearly every booth—if clothing was even the right word for that.

Many of them also had quite an assortment of sex toys.

Most of the people there weren't wearing much, and some even changed into the clothing they were buying right as they put their credit cards away.

Theo and Luca were wearing all black to try and fit the theme since they didn't have any gear. Luckily, Devin had done the same, but for more personal reasons.

"I'm glad you could come. It means a lot when you bother with all my weird interests, Theo."

"You're saying that like I'm not curious about it, too."

"Wait, you are? Why haven't you told me? There's so much I have to show you."

Pulled by the arm, Theo wandered around the vendor market with him. Luca followed close by.

It was nice to see Devin looking better already. There really was something about being engaged in a place that meant so much to you.

At the same time, Theo was trying to calm himself. There wasn't much keeping him from running out of here and chasing down Marco.

"Oh—"

Devin waved into the crowd, and soon enough, another person responded. He then held up his index finger, indicating for them to wait.

"I need to catch up with them. It's been so long. But... One second. Before I leave, I want to say something to you, Theo."

Theo stayed quiet, only giving him a quick nod.

"You know best what needs to be done. I'm not here to tell you to do it, because I don't know if that's the best decision. All I ask is that you give it proper thought before doing anything rash."

"I can't promise anything." There was a tinge of hollowness in Theo's tone.

"Then... At least promise me to take some control back. For once."

Devin didn't wait for an answer. Their eyes lingered on each other for a while as he turned to meet up with his friend.

A hand landed on Theo's shoulder, followed by a whisper, bringing him out of his trance.

"I know you want to rush out. But let's stay a little longer. A break would be good for you."

Continuing through the rest of the indoor area, they hurried through what seemed to be this convention's version of a bar. They ended up passing through that area fairly quickly since it brought back some not-so-welcoming memories.

They also came across a room dedicated to the men who wore what Devin had told him were puppy hoods. There was more to it, but that's all he knew from the one brief exchange they had about it.

The place contained an obstacle course of sorts and cages that some were currently inside.

Theo would be lying if he said he wasn't at least a little intrigued by the men playing around in the ball pit.

The temptation to interact with them was strong, but he held himself back. Luca, however, greeted one with a wave, which made him shake his glove in response. Presumably, that was also a wave, but they couldn't be sure.

What caught their attention next was a large stage. Although nothing was happening on it at the moment, it was likely being set up for later. The surface of it was massive, with large screens covering most of the background. Though currently blank, it was easy to imagine the many colors and lights that would shine there at night.

After heading through numerous dark tunnels, they reached a sign displaying a list of etiquette rules. For a term Theo had never heard of. One of them wasn't a rule, though; it simply stated that they carried both lube, condoms, and gloves.

"Ooh, these are fun." Luca smiled.

Considering the nature of the sign, Theo could only imagine what went on inside the opening it was plastered above.

"What happens in there?"

"You're telling me that that's not obvious?"

"Oh, I think I know. I just want you to say it." Theo's gaze caught Luca off guard, causing his face to heat up under the dim lights.

"A lot of... casual sex. The dark makes it more anonymous."

Neither of them said another word. Their hesitant, shared glances meant enough.

Thin strips of red LED lights lined the section between the walls and the ceiling, providing a minuscule amount of light.

In the darkness, he could primarily discern the other men by their hair. The glow reached some shoulders, but that depended on their height.

Even the man standing in front of him was hard to make out, his most prominent feature being the glinting piercing above his eye.

As the stranger got closer, his head dipped down until the soft touch of his lips pressed against Theo's neck.

Heat rose through his body as a pair of hands felt him up. He sighed but heard the guy beside him match it with an even sweeter moan.

Luca. He must have also found someone.

His sounds were... directing Theo's blood, to say the least. Not to mention, they were getting louder and louder.

"Ugh... Oh, sorry." Louder because Luca was close enough to bump shoulders with him.

Brought out of his daze, Theo looked past the hair of the man by his neck, locking eyes with Luca. The lights shone so brilliantly on his face.

"It's okay... Luca."

The sight of the man entangled with Luca stirred an unfamiliar jealousy in him.

He wanted to push the guy away. To switch places with him. To be the one that made Luca moan like that.

"Theo..."

A third hand slid up his arm.

The man before him backed up once he saw what was happening.

"Yeah?" The hopeful tone in his voice was embarrassingly clear.

"Do you... want to?"

Theo gulped, followed by a slow, deep breath.

"Please..."

They found themselves in a smaller, separate area, which could almost be considered its own room.

Theo's leg knocked against something. A silhouette, its shape and edges blending into the dark. The object looked to be made of leather, catching the faintest glimmer of light on its smooth, glossy surface.

Theo sat on it, leaning back as Luca's knee pressed into the bench between his legs.

Luca had already picked up a tiny bottle and one of the rubber packets offered on a table by the room's entrance. Since the bench was low to the ground, he could easily place them on the floor, and a soft thud sounded as he did.

"You're breathing way too fast. Relax..."

Theo felt something soft prod his lower stomach. As it pressed flat against his skin, he realized it was Luca's hand sliding up under his shirt.

The precise, gentle touch sent a shiver through Theo, his senses attuned to the other man's next move.

"You're making that... very difficult." With his vision impaired, he was more acutely aware of Luca's every action. More sensitive. Every time skin met skin, he sucked in a sharp breath.

"Oh, really? How so?" Luca chuckled as he pushed Theo's shirt further up. It took much longer than Theo would have liked before he pulled it all the way off.

"S-Shh."

With another quiet laugh, Luca fiddled with the rest of Theo's clothes until the cold air hit his fully exposed body.

"Is someone embarrassed?"

Luca's warm hands roamed over every part of him, lingering near his thighs. The contrast in temperature made him squirm.

Such a sensation was new to him, especially since the effects of the darkroom were enhancing it.

"Nnh, shut... up."

Luca brushed his fingers against Theo's cock, causing his body to heat up as his legs trembled.

"Hmm, I can't believe you're still talking back to me like this." Though Luca's voice was steeped in sarcasm, he withdrew his hands from Theo's body, leaving him without even the slightest touch.

"Luca..." Theo whimpered. He heard the faint noise of someone swallowing their own saliva.

From what little he could see of Luca in the weak red glow mixed with the rustling sounds he was making, his best guess was that he was getting his clothes off.

"Patience."

Theo reached his hand out, hoping to make contact with Luca. With some luck, his fingertips grazed the man's stomach.

Light sloshing noises came from him, which, considering the way Luca's body moved, had to be because he was wrapping up and lubing his cock.

"Don't stall." As Theo ran his hand up Luca's body, he heard him breathe in slowly and more manually.

"I... wouldn't dare." There was a tinge of playfulness to his tone, even as he shuddered from Theo's sudden grip on his chest.

"Good..." With a smile, Theo flicked Luca's nipple and twisted it in his fingers.

"Ah—" Luca's body jerked closer, leaning into the touch. One of his hands came down onto the bench, landing next to Theo's head.

"Then, fuck him out of me." Theo reached behind Luca and crept his hand up the back of his thigh.

"Hah..."

He groaned as Theo's fingers dug into his skin.

"I don't want even a sliver of his sweat left on my body." He swiped his palm across Luca's ass, earning him a sweet moan in response. The satisfaction Theo felt just from that was immense.

"Nngh... Sir, yes, sir."

Oh, Luca liked that, did he?

He grabbed Theo by the legs, rubbing his thumbs against his inner thighs. He was teasing him, making it harder for Theo to determine when he'd finally obey.

But... he didn't have to wait long.

A sigh barely escaped Theo before his breath hitched in his throat. Luca had him skewered on his cock with a rough pull of his body.

"F-Fuck." One of Theo's arms fell onto the bench, while the other held tightly onto Luca's arm.

This was already way rougher than he was used to, but it was also exactly what he needed.

It didn't take long for Luca to adjust to Theo's body, learning in record time how to make him cry out in pleasure.

Every slam against his furthest, most sensitive depths was making him arch and quiver from the impact.

Theo didn't find it hard to admit that this man was significantly better than Marco.

"I... wish I could see you better." His grip tightened around Theo's thighs.

"No... I- I look like a mess..."

Theo felt precum leak down his cock as Luca's rhythmic thrusts made his body shudder, a wealth of whimpers and whines escaping him.

His face was practically buried in the leather bench, tears staining the stretched fabric.

"Mmh, a hot one..." Luca's chuckle was enough to heat up the already-burning Theo.

He writhed, an unbearable pressure building up in his lower body.

"O-Oh god, I—" His legs shook and trembled as his eyes rolled back from the sheer ecstasy. Theo's world went dark. It felt as if he merged with the darkroom, becoming one with it.

Mixed with his gasps came another deep moan from the man above him. This one sounded much more final and was accompanied by Luca lingering deep inside him.

"Nnh... fuck..." He dragged himself out of Theo. And before long, exhausted panting filled the room.

The reality of the situation dawned on them. The silence was heavy, but Theo didn't regret his actions.

If anything, he felt so damn good, it was impossible to articulate.

"Luca... You're the best I've ever had."

Chapter 7

Waking up in Luca's apartment felt a little different this time. Mainly, he was actually lying next to him, but it was also tough not to think about last night.

"Luca... I'm going."

The man's eyes opened halfway, and at first, all he did was grunt.

"I appreciate all your help... But it's best if I confront him alone."

"Hold on. Listen... There's no way that's going to go well. Can I at least walk around near his house or something? I'll be able to help if anything goes wrong."

Scooting to the edge of the bed, Theo picked a meowing Briar up from the floor and placed him on his lap.

"That's... fine."

He ruffled its fur, earning a soft purr as Briar leaned against him.

"Theo..."

Fingertips traced Theo's spine. He clutched the cat closer to himself.

"Mmh, yeah?"

"It's a nice thing you're doing for Devin. Ah, and yourself. But... I hope you know what you're getting into." His voice came from beside Theo's ear, close to a whisper.

"Yes."

Theo took a deep breath and made eye contact with the two yellow beads in front of him.

"I do."

They had found a parking lot far from Marco's house but still within walking distance.

Theo was already on his way, glancing back as the car grew smaller. He could no longer see Luca's shadow in the window.

He planned on following from afar.

The closer Theo got, the quicker excuses to run piled up in his head. His footsteps slowed down, and sweat gathered in his palms.

Knowing everything, the house's size felt more intimidating than ever.

Theo stood before the door for at least five minutes until his fist landed on it. A weak knock, if it could even be considered that. His hand opened as his fingers hesitantly tapped on the wood.

It was still possible to leave... He could just head back.

His body reacted negatively to that thought, curling his aggression into another fist. He slammed it so hard against the door that it creaked.

It didn't take long until a tall figure stood before him.

The eerie stare turned into a much less comforting smile.

"Would you like something to drink?"

A chill shot down his spine. Unfortunately, that was a reminder of why he was even here in the first place—his best friend.

"I'll make it myself. Thank you."

Marco's eye twitched, but he stepped to the side, letting Theo walk past him.

He heard the door close but not lock. That should mean easy access for Luca.

As Theo made it to the kitchen, his gaze landed on the knife lying on the counter.

He searched through every cupboard, finding the instant coffee he was looking for. This shouldn't take long.

"I have a machine. Use it. That stuff is just for emergency situations."

When he turned his head, he saw Marco standing in the doorway.

"I don't mind. You can keep your capsules or grounds or whatever."

Marco's eyebrows drew together.

"Your lip. The wound is almost gone."

Mug.

"Mhm. Good observation."

Powder.

"No need to be so cold, Theo. You're here of your own accord, aren't you?"

Water and a kettle.

"Yes. You get that it's not because I'm forgiving you, right?"

"Awh, really? I was hoping for a loving reconciliation."

"If that wasn't sarcasm, you're more delusional than I thought."

A ding. The water was done heating.

"You can't judge me for thinking there might be a chance to fix this."

As he poured water into the mug, Theo could hear the floorboards creak, echoing Marco's footsteps.

His heart dropped.

"Marco..."

The other man's hands shot out, his fingers wrapping around Theo's throat with a vice-like grip.

"Yes, love?"

Panic surged as he raked at Marco's hands, trying to free himself.

Theo's vision blurred, wheezing gasps struggling to escape him.

"You know, I prefer this. It would be much better if you just stayed quiet."

Recalling the first thing he noticed upon entering Marco's kitchen, he let go with one hand and reached for the counter. His fingers stretched and trembled, straining for the lifeline.

Theo's flicker of hope ignited as his fingertips brushed against the cold metal.

"Wait—"

His hand closed around the large knife's handle. Summoning his remaining strength, he swung the blade upward. Marco's grip loosened for a split second, a startled grunt escaping him.

Gasping for breath, Theo held the blade to his chest, forcing him to step back.

"I wish... I knew what to say to you. But... This is just too insane."

"Please. Calm down." Marco traced his hand up Theo's arm, surprisingly unbothered by the sharp edge slicing into his shirt.

"Stop touching me."

He didn't move, making Theo tighten his grip on the knife.

"Theo... You can't just give up. We could... be something. Something good."

He shoved the blade forward, feeling the tip connect with soft flesh. Marco's breath hitched, and he finally let go.

"With me as some kind of silent puppet or something? Who loves you unconditionally?"

"Okay, I'm sorry about that. It... won't happen again."

"Wow, more lies. You'd do better with a therapist for a lover."

Hurried footsteps echoed from the entrance, growing louder once they reached the kitchen floorboards. He was here.

"Theo, you can relax. I'll help you deal with this monster."

Marco only briefly glanced at him, scorn in his eyes.

"Stay with me. Come... here." He held his arms out, inviting Theo closer.

An overwhelming cluster of thoughts flooded his mind, containing scarring imagery of what could have gone down between Marco and Devin.

The last reminder to finally make him snap.

"Go to hell, Marco."

He thrust his blade forward, plunging it deep into Marco's chest.

The impact was swift, causing a flash of searing pain that stole Marco's breath as he stumbled back against the wall.

And yet, much to Theo's dismay, he smiled.

"Ugh, yes... There's no better way to go..."

Gritting his teeth, Theo twisted the knife, making himself shudder from the grotesque sound of his skin tearing open.

It didn't work.

After every cough and choke, every drop, and every line of blood that leaked out of his mouth or stained his shirt, Marco's lips stretched further. One could even confuse his grunts for moans if they were twisted enough.

"Don't look at me like that."

He knew what to do. Yanking the weapon back out, Theo turned his eyes to Luca, who was staring wide-eyed at them.

He threw the thing to the other end of the room so a staggering Marco couldn't possibly attain it. Theo then headed toward Luca as his victim slumped to the floor.

"You didn't... have to go that far." His back bumped against the wooden doorway as Theo forced himself inside the narrow entrance.

Theo noted his flushed cheeks with interest.

"Are you getting hard?"

Luca had a tough time looking him in the eyes.

"It's... nice to see someone finally fight back against him. But..."

"And?" Theo cut in.

"No, not—"

"And?"

Luca sighed.

"How you're acting right now is kind of... hot."

Pressing their bodies closer together, Theo kneaded his knee into the growing shape in Luca's pants.

"You're sick, you know that?" Theo's smile widened as the man before him writhed and whimpered.

"Nngh..."

Directing his smile at Marco, he saw the opposite: a frown and a struggle for breath.

It worked.

"Why are you scowling at me?"

"Stop. Get away from him. That's not... Gh—how it's meant to be." Marco's voice was hoarse. His body collapsed onto the floor as he dragged himself by the arms towards them.

But he didn't get far. Blood pooled out under him, and all he could do was let out a weak grunt.

"What have I done...?" Luca barely managed a whisper. His body meekly arched, grinding against Theo's steady leg.

Theo found it amusing that even after such a brutal display, Luca was still somewhere else entirely.

His question, however, Theo was keen on dismissing.

"Nothing." Theo leaned his face down to the man's neck, tracing his tongue in a long, wet line up his skin. With a needy sigh, Luca trembled as he grabbed his arm.

"Can we... do this somewhere else? I can't look at him anymore."

"Mmh... Sure."

It felt wrong being in Marco's bedroom after all that. There were so many reasons Theo couldn't possibly count them all. Some of which he didn't even understand himself. Only Luca could.

Luca... The handsome man splayed out naked on the linen bed sheets below.

Theo ran his hand through Luca's hair, scratching the back of his head. The overtly pleased groan and closed eyes seemed to Theo like a desperate need to hide from what he had witnessed. He was more than willing to offer Luca as much.

As Theo leaned closer, Luca's lips parted before him.

"Want it, huh?" Theo spoke under his breath, closing the gap between their mouths. Luca responded in kind with a soft whimper.

Their tongues connected as Theo's fingers dug deeper into his hair.

He trailed his free hand down Luca's stomach, coming to a stop just below the navel.

Luca sucked in a sharp breath, which halted his tongue. Theo's hand, however, advanced again, slowly wrapping around the part of him that was still begging for attention. Theo teased him, pressing his thumb against the sensitive head of Luca's cock.

Luca gasped and broke away from the kiss. He pushed his face into the pillow, trying to muffle his moans.

"Look at me." Theo got a firmer grip on Luca's whole length but only moved in slow strokes.

It gave Luca the space to compose himself, but that wasn't necessarily what he wanted.

"Please... Nnh—Just... fuck me."

Theo's face heated up as he hurried to get his fingers out of Luca's hair and into the nightstand drawer. He'd been here before; he knew where the lube was.

"You're... more submissive than I thought."

Taking the bottle out, he let go of Luca to slather himself in it, eliciting a soft whine from him.

"S-Stop teasing me..."

Theo merely smiled, placing one hand on Luca's thigh and the other on his own cock.

Easier able to direct himself like this, he entered the other man with a satisfied sigh.

Luca arched, his groan shifting from ragged and painful to one of bliss as Theo reached the deepest part of him.

"Nnh... So beautiful..." He drove his fingers through Luca's hair once again. This time, he grasped it roughly and yanked his head back.

Luca's reactions to every thrust heightened. He writhed against the bedsheets, struggling to figure out which parts of the fabric to grab onto.

Theo couldn't remember the last time he had felt a man wrapped around his cock. All he recalled was that he didn't have close to as much control back then as he did now.

Now, he was the one taking charge. And it was the best goddamn feeling, especially after securing revenge for the most important person in his life.

Theo's hand came up, joining the other one by Luca's neck, as he gently wrapped his fingers around him.

"Gh—Theo... H-Harder..."

He avoided pressing down on anything that would cause real damage but strengthened his grip on Luca's throat.

Luca tightened around Theo's cock, which only made him hasten his thrusts, desperate for more of that eager response.

"Yes... Good..."

The man whimpered and gasped below him, the friction between their bodies getting increasingly intense. Theo felt an overwhelming pressure building up inside him. He was reaching the edge. And considering the precum coating Luca's cock, so was he.

He enjoyed so immensely the sight of Luca convulsing in his grip, but wanting to gain more control over where they were headed, his hands returned to Luca's thighs.

In his heated rhythm, Theo went as deep as he could, noting the aftermath of the choking. Luca's eyes were blurred by tears, and his moans came out more raspy.

"I-I—Fuck..."

As if on cue, and with every nerve on fire, the tension in Theo was released. He groaned, painting the other man's insides white.

At that moment, the same opaque liquid dribbled down Luca's cock while his body lurched, and a soundless gasp escaped him.

Theo dragged himself out of the disheveled mess of a person, looking him over carefully. A perfect sight, Theo would easily consider art. But then again, his mind wasn't all there right now.

He collapsed onto the bed next to Luca. With a faint smile, Theo nestled against his body, curling up to him.

Two exhausted people entangled in each other's arms. So, very exhausted.

It was over. It was all over. Especially, for the man known as Theodore.

She looked so frail standing there. Even more than usual. Audrey's head was held low to the ground as she waited for her son to break the silence.

"You look shaken up. Did something happen?"

Her lips stayed in a thin line. When she finally looked back at him, her gentle eyes were filled with an uncomfortable level of suspicion.

"Come in. I'll explain." She turned around, fiddled with the rim of her shirt, and disappeared through the first door on her right.

Theo stared at the entrance hall's many photographs. Every family member had their own frame, except for him and Silas. They hung there twice, with both a young and an old version.

He'd like to say he felt... anything. But, no.

Audrey almost never sat in the chair opposite her living room table. She usually joined him on the couch, but not this time.

"Someone... came to my house. A while back. He didn't want to tell me his name. My life—Theo—was threatened because of you. I want to hope it wasn't your fault, but... I don't know anymore." Tears welled up in her eyes.

Theo still felt nothing. Except for a knot in his stomach.

"I'm... sorry." An underwhelming response. But he didn't know what else to say.

Audrey gulped, glancing off to the side.

"Silas. He... had to get treated for a cat bite." She paused, somehow giving herself whiplash from the topic shift.

"He thought he was a bit too cool at first and let it go untreated for too long. I had to help get him to the doctor."

Silas was in a weaker state than usual. Interesting.

"Oh."

"It wasn't... Briar, was it?"

"I'm... so sorry." Lifelessly, Theo pulled his phone out.

Audrey watched, clutching the arm of the chair as he put it to his ear. "Silas?"

"What the fuck do you want? I said it's over."

"I just want to meet up one more time."

Silence.

"You can accept that, can't you? It won't be long, I promise."

He knew. He knew something was different. Theo never talked like this. In this manner. This tone.

Audrey knew. Her face contorted. However, she didn't say or do anything. She didn't even try to stop him.

"Damn. Still being polite, I see. To be honest, there might be some courage in that."

A low, throaty laugh came from Theo.

"So?"

"Why not. Come over. Show me what you learned."

Theo smiled.

"I can't wait."